HIBA KOUEIFI

Jasmine's refuge

Inspired by stories of Syrian refugees in the West

Some people give from their hearts...
excuses from their love...
support from their bright smile...
Anna Marie Tempero is one of them
I was lucky to meet her
To her, I dedicate this book

Contents

One

FAREWELL

❦

It's about time! I just started to write my diary. I like to write about things I experience; writing about memories is something new for me. I began to write as I promised my Teta[1] when we left our home country, Syria, heading to America; "the Dream Land" for many people, or "the Land of Uncle Sam" as many nicknamed it in various stories we have read but actually it was the "Escape Land" for us.

It was the last night before leaving. There were a lot of visitors; family members, neighbors, and friends who came to deliver us a last goodbye. My family and I were thrilled because we were going to have a new experience in the United States. However, it was hard for all of us to leave our spirits behind. My lovely grandparents, cousins, friends, photos, a our home, where we spent the most beautiful times of o I will miss them a lot.

Later, all visitors left, except my grandparent

1

Sami who was going to drive us to the airport. Actually, we were in my grandparents' home. My family's house was located in a dangerous region, where the war is taking place. Since the war started, the conditions got worse, so we moved to my father's parents' home that was in a safer area. My mother's parents used to live in Homs; another city in Syria, before they moved to Germany a few months back.

As soon as the visitors left, I found myself wandering around the house, reflecting on a lot of details in it as I hadn't done before. It was a warm winter's day; all of us were sitting outside in the "sky space" (or the courtyard in the literal translation). It was found in the Syrian old houses style and located in the middle of the house. I like this place; it is big enough to let the family and visitors feel comfortable in the fresh air. It also provides privacy and does not disturb neighbors. In the middle of the "sky space" there is a water fountain and two trees; lemon and a Jasmine bush which is as big as a tree. There are a lot of green plant pots everywhere as well. Here we used to enjoy sharing the full moon in our family get-together meetings.

I stopped next to my Jasmine[2] tree; my favorite flower. My dad planted it when he was a child, and he was still taking care for it. He even named me after its name. I feel that the Jasmine tree loves me as I love it. I touched its branches, smelled its wonderful scent, and picked up some flowers of it to take them with me in a nice small box. Jasmine flower is considered as a Damascus symbol. It is found in the majority of the Damascus Arabic houses, and outside the regular houses on the road sides. People enjoy the evening breeze carrying Jasmine fragrance while they are around.

Rooms are surrounding the sky area. Each room has a window facing the sky area, and another one facing the road.

Rooms are big with high ceilings and tall windows. The main house door is solid, big and wider than the internal ones.

Perhaps, it was the first time I realized these details. This reflection drove me to remember and feel every word of the poem we had learned in the third-grade class:

> *"My home's ceiling is made up of iron*
> *My home's sides are made up of stone*
> *Oh wind blow strongly, oh rain cry hard*
> *I am not afraid of wind nor danger."*

Mom, Dad and "Jiddo"[3] were making the final touches; preparing things, closing the luggage, and putting them in the car with Sami's help. At the same time, my brother Majd, my sister Amal, and I were sitting around Teta as we usually do when she wants to tell us one of her beautiful old tales. In fact, she stayed with us to be sure that we remember her advice about being careful and taking care of each other and our parents.

"Kids, we still have about four hours before leaving. We should move at five a.m. You should sleep to get some rest. We have a long trip."

Mom said. All of us were tired, but no one of us wanted to sleep.

As she whispered to each of Majd and Amal in their ears the personal advice, Teta lengthily hugged and kissed them, then she did the same with me.

"Oh, beautiful young lady, you are going to be 16 years old in two months. I know you are very sensitive. Don't give in to any sad thoughts, let those thoughts pass quickly, be strong, think positively and say "boukra-ahla."[4] Please honey, on a nice notebook write down anything that happens to you; feelings,

3

thoughts, memories, or anything you want to talk about. Keep these notes for yourself, or maybe for your future kids."

Teta whispered into my ear and then said: "promise?" in tears mixed with a smile, I replied: "Promise! That's a great idea! I also will save it for you Teta."

The sky area in an old house where the family used to gather

Two

ANOTHER PLANET

During the trip, we changed airplanes more than one time. Last flight, I sat next to the window. I wanted to see the scene of my new homeland from above. It was sunset when the airplane got close to the ground, and the view got clearer. The view was adorable! I saw high buildings and rivers; it seemed like it was Pittsburgh City.

I also realized that there were two different regions within the city; groups of beautiful houses surrounded by trees in a wonderful organized style with dim lights. The other region is like a wide open space with more lights and a lot of advertisement panels. The two areas look different and separate from each other. The open spaces are market plazas, as I knew later from my dad.

After the plane landed and the official procedures got done at the airport, a lady was waiting for us. She represents the organization that takes care of refugees. She drove us to the house that was prepared for us.

"Yasmine. Yasmine, wake up! Come on, look!! The snow is all over the place". Amal shouted! It took me a while to notice where I was. It is a different place, a different feeling. Oh, yes, we are here in America. I didn't realize how we got home. The last thing I could remember was when I got into the car after we left the airport. I was drained. Amal called me again. I got up and headed to her near the window. What a beautiful view! Everything all around was white; the wonderful neighborhood was covered with snow, and it was still snowing. Amazing! I like the snow very much. We used to go to the mountain to enjoy playing with snow, but it is adorable watching while sitting inside; safe and warm.

Mom came to join us on our first morning in America, then dad and Majd came as well. We were all happy to have some quiet minutes this morning after the stressful time we had in the past few days. I had a feeling that each one of us was drowned into his own reflections, but not for long! Amal, my 11- year old sister, couldn't keep calm any longer. She started jumping, moving around, and talking: "Look here, look there, what is this? What is that…?", she began her discovery journey all around the house. Her words prompted us to explore the house, too.

The house was beautiful but old. It needed to get some fixes and clean up. Our luggage was on the floor, some were unpacked with a lot of mess. There were many things new to us. The house was in an old building that had just two floors; each floor had four apartments. The house main door looked like any inside door, and it had a doorknob from both sides; in and out. The floor was made up of wood. When you walk, you feel the ground moving under your feet, and squeaking.

ANOTHER PLANET

The house had two bedrooms, a sitting room with a corner like a small room, a bathroom, and a small kitchen located in the middle of the house. The kitchen had an oven and a refrigerator. The bedrooms already had built-in closets. The house had some furniture that was old but necessary, such as a sofa and three beds. I liked my new home.

"Come to eat!" Mom called. It's almost noon, we were hungry. There were some bread, cheese, milk, olives, and two cereal boxes, which my parents bought yesterday on the way back from the airport. Amal, Majd, and I wanted to eat cereal with milk. We were excited to have our breakfast as American people do. There were no bowls and we used plastic cups instead.

A few minutes later, my dad said:"Samia is here," while he looked out the window. She was the "airport lady." She and my parents agreed to meet today. Her mission was to guide the refugees and help them to reach their needs in this new life.

She was tall, slim, with brown hair and hazel eyes. Her skin had the color of "wheat", with some deep wrinkles, especially on her forehead; she looked older than my mother.

Samia and my parents sat in the living room. We sat in the kitchen eating while listening to the conversation because they were talking in Arabic. With her weak and different Arabic accent, she told them that she was American with Arabic roots; she was originally from Iraq.

They spent more than one hour discussing and explaining a lot of issues; school, work, transportation, grocery, and many other things. My mom went into small details as she always does; worry about everything.

Jasmine's refuge

A style of an old Syrian main door

Three

PASSING BARRIERS

The first few months were the hardest time we had in this country. The bus stop was close to our home, which made it easy to go for grocery shopping and to other places. We lost our way a few times before we got experienced in how to deal with this matter.

The public education system in Syria is almost free including the higher education. It was a good chance for my parents. My dad had a chemistry diploma. He used to work in a food factory in Syria.

Now, he got a job at a pizza shop not so far from the house. He couldn't find a better job matching with his specialty, because that needs some equivalency procedures, like studying and passing difficult exams to get a license to work in his field. At the same time, he started preparing to get a driver's license.

Chores were a big issue. It was already my mom's passion for making the home extra clean and neat. All of us worked hard in the first week to clean the house under mom's supervision. My 18-year old brother, Majd, worked with my dad to do miscellaneous things that needed fixing around the house. We cleaned up each inch in the house. The hardest one was cleaning the carpet. Aunt Samia lent us a carpet cleaning machine, but my mom washed the carpet one more time by rubbing it with a cloth by her hands.

The very thing that bothered my mom most was that there was no drainer in the bathroom or kitchen as we had in our home country. We used to clean the home by washing with soap and water, then driving the dirty water to the drainer in the kitchen or bathroom. Here, dad used to keep reminding us not to throw water on the floor in the bathroom or anywhere inside the home. That was strange to us.

There was no washing machine in the house. All laundry should be taken to the laundry shop. In my country, those shops are run by experts to iron clothes, dry cleaning, or to clean kinds of clothes that need special care such as blankets. In the first few months, we used to hear mom nagging a lot because of this issue.

My mother holds an Arabic language diploma, but she did not have a job. As the majority of women in our country, mom's choice was to have more time for taking care, and cooking for us; she counted those things as her priority. Traditionally, she liked keeping up with the family members, and spending time with friends.

My mom once told me that women in Arabic culture don't have to work to get money; it is the man's responsibility. In the past, it was considered to be shameful for the man if the woman was contributing financially to the family. Culture changes with time. Recently, in our country, many women prefer to work to support their families or improve their community.

We attended school, which was another tragedy and funny story. Many things about the school here were different. Schools here are beautiful, and big with wonderful yards that opened to the road. Students could practice many kinds of athletic activities. Students didn't have one classroom for all the subject areas as we used to have in Syria. Here we follow the teachers' classrooms according to the subjects.

We studied English as a second language in our home country, but not enough to use or understand what people say because they were talking fast and using the informal language. That led to many funny and embarrassing situations. Sometimes, I felt tired of hearing English talks, because I should stay focused and alert all the time to keep up with the conversation. However, I found listening better than talking; it was like someone had a stone in his throat preventing words from getting out of his lips.

In the morning of the first day of school, when each one of the students had to go to their classroom, my sister was crying because she was scared to leave me and go to her classroom. She was frightened to be alone with new people because she didn't know how to talk and communicate with them.

Even though Amal has a strong personality, she was still young to control herself in such situations. She usually doesn't cry unless there is something harsh impacting her. I thought that I knew and understood her feelings, because it was a hard day for me too. Some bad thoughts came to my mind, such as "The playground is open, what if she thought that she could go home alone." This thought overwhelmed me. I couldn't wait anymore, I ran to her to tell her that everything will be okay, and to remind her that I am here with her in the same school, I

11

wanted her to calm down.

Things got worse when the teacher prevented me from leaving my class group. I uselessly tried to explain what I wanted to do. I just wanted a few minutes to talk with my sister to comfort her. But because I was nervous and confused, words were jumbling in my head and I started crying. In this complicated moment, a girl of my age came and talked to me in a weak Arabic language. She helped us to solve this problem peacefully.

Jasmine flowers

Four

THE MOON SMILE

I thought that my first day at school will be the worst of this new life. I found out that it turned out to be the best one. Sometimes goodness comes after difficulty as they say. Now, I have got a new friend. Noura is the nicest and the most helpful girl who saved me that day and on many other occasions. Our friendship got stronger as the days passed by at school.

Noura is American. She was born and grew up here in Pittsburgh. Her dad is a dentist, originally from Syria. He came a long time ago to America to study. Noura's mom is a science teacher who is originally American. Noura has a younger brother named Adam. She and her family used to visit Syria every summer before the war had started. Noura still has beautiful memories about the days she spent there. From her mother's side, she only has a grandmother who lives close to them. I happily accompanied Noura to visit her several times. Visiting her took me on a journey in time and place, because

13

her home seems to have a story in each corner. It reminds me of my Teta's home. It's warmly old, and I can smell the fragrance of past years.

She offered us some tasty home-made cookies that reminded me of my Teta when she used to save nuts and dried fruits in a cabinet in her room to give to all her grandchildren when they visited her.

Despite the cultural differences, it seems that Noura's Teta and mine have things in common. She told us that she lived in a conservative community, when wearing pants was considered shameful. She is a strong lady because she faced the obstacles bravely until she won.

During her university education, she was one of two girls in the chemistry class. A girl being in a university at that time was unacceptable. I am sure it is a hard challenge for a girl at that age. I enjoy visiting her and listening to her talks.

Day after day, our friendship got stronger and more tight. I enjoyed spending time with her, exchanging our news and experience. Really, she was a good source of knowledge about American culture and habits. I thought that I knew a lot of American lifestyle that I had learned via movies and books, but I realized that I almost knew nothing; things in reality are different.

Noura was always interested to hear anything about our country and culture. We somehow look similar in our characters and hobbies. The most common hobby we have is listening to famous Arabic music.

Actually, when it comes to music, I found that there were some differences in this subject regarding not just rhythm or instruments. It was related to how people interact and get involved with the music. Maybe the life style is the reason, or the lyrics and type of music. My family, like most neighbors and people in Syria, are used to spend the morning coffee time listening to calm songs. The music was for very famous singers, especially Fayrouz; the most renowned singer in the whole Arabic world. You can enjoy listening to the same song while walking in the narrow neighborhoods, because houses were so close almost as if they were hugging each other. Music sneaks into your ears. Most radio channels play the same type of songs.

> *I'll pick up for you this time*
>   *just this time*
>   *early in the morning*
>   *just early in the morning*
>   *any red flower*
>   *I don't want more*

This, I think, is the famous one. It used to use as the introduction segment of the "Welcome Morning" program.

Sometimes I feel that I want to hide in my room or somewhere to stay alone listening to my favorite songs to release my deep emotions, to reflect, remember, and also cry. Today, when I came back from school, I remembered my old home in Syria. I felt sorry to leave it behind and ran away. I missed it a lot.

It was a big one of six apartments in a three-floor building. It is the new Syrian houses style. As kids, we were happy to deliver a delicious dish of meal or dessert to neighbors due to an old habit. This was a tradition followed by all the neighbors.

Jasmine's refuge

A neighborhood in old Damascus

Five

THE BIG MEETING

More days and weeks had passed since we got to the United States of America. Things ran slowly, there was no big change. Samia still visited us every once in a while to support and offer her help. The last thing she told us was about a refugees' meeting next Sunday at the nearest Mosque organized by the Mosque members.

We were so excited to hear this news. We were looking forward to meeting people who speak our language and share similar memories about many things. When people have the same background, they could understand and accept us the way we are. I am sure we must have faced similar circumstances. Noura happily told me that she and her family will be there. Her parents were part of the organizing team. We wanted our families to meet each other.

Finally, the awaited day had come. We were so excited. We spent the last few days talking and building expectations. Dad wanted to get more information about job opportunities to improve his income. Mom was interested in learning about Arabic food shops. She also wanted to know how to deal with some struggles like the paperwork she received from the school. My sister, brother, and I were expecting to have more new friends.

We dressed up very well. Samia came to pick us up to the party. There were a lot of people, most of them were Americans but originally from Arabic and East Asian countries. The warm welcome all refugees had received broke the ice wall that was hidden inside each one of us. The event had a formal beginning; a welcome speech with some important points to be known for the refugee community.

The welcome speech was important and interesting for senior people because it gave them information about questions they were seeking answers for. It took a long time to discuss and explain how to deal with things like governmental processes, booking appointments, applying for jobs, etc.

Cash and credit card usage for payment was the most important subject to discuss. Usually, people in Syria used cash only for payments. Interaction with banks was minimal compared with the US.

The speaker pointed out that this talk was just to highlight the most important subjects, and there would be more meetings to follow up with things.

Anyways, this part was boring for us as kids. Noura with her brother, my brother, Amal, and I slowly got out to the yard. We sat down on benches we found outside in the big yard. It was a little cold, even though it was a sunny day. People were still coming to the party, some kids in our age joined us to stay outside. Noura knew some of them; Kareem from Dara'a

City, Lina from Aleppo City, and Wafaa from Damascus, the capital. They were from different regions of Syria. There were some differences somehow between all of us, because of the geographic and environmental factors. Yet, all Syrian cities approximately have similar culture and beliefs.

We had a long exciting talk. Each one had a different story he or she had lived or heard. Most stories talked about hard times with strange details. The strangest and interesting story was Kareem's. He told us about a man from his region who was stuck in Kuala Lumpur airport for seven months before he had a help from a Canadian lady who heard about his case. He had never met her before. His legal papers to stay in Malaysia expired, so he tried to go somewhere else, but no country gave him permission to allow him in. His story is available on YouTube. His experience is the real version of "The Terminal" movie.

Lina told us another story about her uncle and his family of five kids. They lived in a major contributed city in the Syrian; Aleppo economy. It had a lot of big factories. Lina's uncle and two of his sons used to work in one of them. They worked hard for a long time until they could buy a small home. During the war, one unfortunate day, his two sons went to their jobs, but they never came back. The factory was totally destroyed by a sudden attack. The father was saved by chance because he was busy in another place. It was a big shock to him and the whole family. He blamed himself because he insisted on staying in the country to settle down in his lovely home, where he wanted to spend the rest of his life. He hoped that the war was going to end soon. Now, he found that he was forced to leave the region because things were getting worse. His wife was heartbroken, sad, scared, and worried. She and the children could not bear to hear the bombs roaring outside. Because he had no money, no proper education, and no ability to start over, he decided to go to a camp in Turkey. It is the nearest country to Aleppo, which was the only choice he had. They could carry just the essential things as he was informed, because there was not enough room in the tent; their new home. Each one of the family chose a special thing to take with his stuff. Kids took some of their books and toys. The father took the Damask rose[5] pot, the smallest one he already planted in sand from his yard. The mother took photos of her missing sons. That was all what they had to start a new life in a tent which didn't protect them from the cold winter or the hot summer.

The Damask Rosa

Six

FAMILY NIGHT

~ ❧❦❧ ~

We got back home with uncle Samir and his family; dad's new friend. He insisted on driving us home. From their conversation on the way back, I realized that they had things in common. Damascus was their home city, and they used to go to the same school but uncle Samir is older than my dad.

Uncle Samir and his family came to the US a few years ago. They came as regular immigrants seeking a better life, and they had individuals of their family already living here.

Even though the stories I heard yesterday made me sad and upset, that Sunday was a very interesting day for all of us. When we got home, there were many subjects to talk about. Each one of us had questions, stories, comments, and a lot of things we noticed or details to discuss. The most important thing for me was the meeting between Noura's family and mine. Our mothers set up for a visit soon.

Later in the evening, the whole family sat down together to

drink tea as usual, but today we had many things to talk about. My father was delighted to meet uncle Samir.

"He knew well what I need and wonder about, because he had the same experiences," Dad said. Agreeing with him, mom said: "I have met and talked to a variety of ladies, and I've got along with Samir's wife."

Amal couldn't wait more; she wanted to talk about her new friend Mariam, uncle Samir's daughter.

"Mariam knows many interesting places where we could play and have fun, and we should go to those places soon," roared Amal.

Majd met a number of boys of his age, but he didn't make friendship with anyone. When my dad asked him about that, he said: "I couldn't find a distinct friend to share with him my hobbies or interesting things, but I had enjoyed talking with all of them."

Mom told us that my grandparents were going to join us from Germany online via Skype right now. All of us were glad and enthusiastic to hear from them. After exchanging greetings, my grandmother added news about a relative she knows who was pregnant. The lady, her husband and their two children used to live in a dangerous area before her husband left to Germany. He went to look and prepare for a better life for the family. At the same time, she and her kids moved to Lebanon, the nearest country to them to stay with her sister- in-law.

In Germany, her husband had gotten some help from the government and friends to establish a good living condition. He worked hard uselessly to process his family legal papers to join him, because of new strict regulations against new comers. At this time, she was suffering from the similar regulations that force Syrian people to get out and re-enter Lebanon every fifteen days to stay legal; otherwise, they will be deported. This caused a big problem for her and her kids, physically and financially.

The obstacles she had were really driving her into a deep depression. She decided to join her husband whatever the cost would be. The only way she had, was to go through the sea "illegally."

"What a crazy decision especially for a pregnant woman with two children! Did she have any dependable company?" My mother asked. The answer was, "an eighteen- year-old person from her neighborhood crossed the sea with her until they reached the European coast. Then he had a different destination he had to take. She was in her ninth month of pregnancy and wanted to arrive before she got her new baby."

"How could she continue her trip? She didn't know the German language!" Mom asked.

"During the journey, she kept communicating with her sister, who already lives in Germany as well." Teta replied, and continued: "She didn't trust anybody who she didn't already know, and she tried to avoid asking for help as much as she could due to the hard times she had experienced which taught her to be careful. She hid a small knife in her pocket to defend herself and her kids if required, and she told the kids to refuse any kind of food or candy offered from strangers.""Incredible! Now I can imagine how horribly she was afraid." My father wondered.

"Finally, she had to ask for help following her sister's advice, when her cell phone battery almost died. She asked someone who looked like a kind person for help. Her sister talked to him and offered to pay him all the cost he needed to help her reach her destination. Kindly, the man did his best until she reached her family safely. One week later, she got her new baby."

At the end of the story, my imagination went directly away to retrieve the feeling of a song that was an introduction of a TV series we lately used to watch. It says:

Take me away to any country
Leave me... forget me
In the ocean.. dump me
Don't ask
I don't have any other way
I am not going to enjoy or relax
By war, My home, was collapsed
And by its smoke I was bitterly hurt

A view from Latakia city on the Syrian coast

FAMILY NIGHT

Seven

FUNNY MISTAKES

With each passing day, there was always at least a new thing to talk about, and to extend our experience. Keeping in touch with people was the best way to open new horizons of knowledge and understanding between our new community and us. Otherwise, all known things were shallow. In fact, interacting with people had many challenges because of the differences in culture, language, and habits.

Improving the English language was one of the subjects discussed at the last event on Sunday. Learning the language was identified as the first and most important step to do before anything. There was a variety of choices to achieve this point. There were afternoon school classes set up by public schools, special classes set up by nonprofit organizations, and private classes offered online or in the newspaper advertisement. Besides teaching language, classes like this help managing social matters, and ease understanding of the new social life.

FUNNY MISTAKES

This program was designed for adults and older people who didn't attend school. For my dad, his job was a good place to gain language skills; in addition, he had some good background experience. Only mom needed to attend classes like those. The experience she had already gotten at school wasn't enough to get a job or at least to do her things without asking for help. Practicing real life was the best way to reach this goal. All of us made grammar mistakes or said awkward sentences, but in most cases she was making funny mistakes by translating or spelling words that give different meanings.

My mother was very interested in this class that had finally started. To enroll, she took a placement test to decide her level of learning. The class was to take place in the neighborhood public library twice a week. The first meeting was fascinating because mom felt that she put her foot on the right track.

That evening, our family discussion was about mom's new class. The surprising news was that mom was the only student in the class! This case pushed her to do her best because all focus was just on her. Later, mom used to tell us all the new and special things she had learned about the culture or local habits. The most interesting thing we enjoyed listening to was mom's language mistakes. One day, the tutor asked her to talk about food.

"I prefer vegetable and healthy food, but I really enjoy eating snakes," my mother said.

"Snakes? Healthy food!! How do you eat it?" The tutor asked strangely.

"Yeah, I know it's unhealthy, and it ruins my diet, but I can't hold myself from sharing my kids when they are eating."

"Your kids?"

Mom realized that there was something wrong. She opened

her purse and pulled out a small bag while she said: "I have some here." At this moment, the tutor was ready to jump away before she saw a chocolate bar and some candies. "You mean snacks!" She said while she burst with laughter.

"I suppose the teacher thought that you and the whole family are wild people who enjoy eating snakes."

Majd said laughingly, and he continued telling a new joke he had:

"There was a new immigrant who wanted to rent a house. He was checking and asking about everything.

"Is there a wife available in this house mister"? He asked the owner.

"What?" The owner replied.

"Yes, I need a wife. Wife is very important, mister, do you have one, mister?"

"Yes, I have."

"How do you got your wife, mister? So I can apply for a wife to me?"

"Apply? How I..? I don't understand! Is this the way you got married?"

"Who talked about marriage? I want a wife to do my work and classes on-line."

" Oh, you mean Wi-Fi."

"What! That is terrible! I cannot bear it anymore. I do not want to talk or say anything; I am going to stay at home. I do not want to find myself in situations like this." Mom said.

"It is just a joke mom!" Replied Majd.

"However, people here are very nice, and helpful. Mostly, they understand the situation and they don't make a direct judgment. We should keep going forward bravely and carefully." Dad commented.

FUNNY MISTAKES

Tea is one of Syrian traditional
beverages

Eight

SPOTLIGHTS

Anyhow, we felt better because we got engaged in our new life, and we were able to manage our things. Each day, one of us had to nag about something, usually about funny, embarrassing, and sad situations that we face.

This weekend was terrific, and I waited for it happily. We were invited to spend this Saturday at Noura's home and enjoy the barbecue. Mom made a traditional delicious meal and also a kind of dessert to take with us.

We had a lot of fun mixed with happiness and memories, because it reminded me of the family gatherings we used to do every weekend at my grandparent's home. However, today was useful and important, because there was a long discussion about the different cultural habits and experiences that we face every day in this new country.

Some of the topics that our discussions touched on included discrimination towards some refugees. The root of this issue might be because our background and personality were different. However, like all other people, our community includes behaved and misbehaved families due to differences in raising the individuals. This is true about all communities, no matter where you are from. There are some actions most of us used to do that are considered unacceptable. Some of these actions include; talking loudly on the cell phone in public places, interrupting other people while talking, not giving enough space for passing pedestrians, using the horn, etc.. I know that these habits have to be adjusted.

On the other hand, some beliefs are not easy to abandon for example adoption or wearing style.

"Oh! Notice that you do not have to change your thoughts, beliefs or culture to manage with your new life. The constitution has saved important rights as religion and speech rights. You just have to manage your actions to fit the situation or at least to show that you respect the others' beliefs or life style." Noura's mom said.

"You are right! I have heard that at Mosque meeting and from my boss at work, but still there are some cases we consider as terrible ones. For example, taking kids away from their parents based on bad treatment is a very strange matter, and against our beliefs and culture. This case happens in our country in infrequent situations only if bad treatment was clearly proven. However, in cases like this, kids were given to a special institution if there was no relative available to take care of them, but do not end up being adopted, and would still get to see their parents".

It was a long discussion about this and other subjects. I realized how much this matter was sensitive, especially when they told a real story about requesting to take a girl away from her parents because she was smaller than she should be at her age even though she was in good health. This complaint was presented to the court by the girl's doctor. Fortunately, the case was rejected because the lawyer proved that the parents and their ancestors were inherently small in size, and they were good parents.

All of us were following this conversation carefully; our parents wanted us to hear this important subject to be aware of how things worked in this country.

Majd gave Amal a teasing look and said: "Be careful [Fashkoula][6] otherwise you will go to live with another family."

"I am not fashkoula!", Amal replied loudly and tried to hide her fear.

"I am just kidding Ammoula. You are getting older and wiser, sweetie."

"If someone does not like pets or feels scared of dogs, and shows that to the pet's owner; is that wrong or impolite?"

Majd asked, and everybody understood that he meant Amal!

"Actually, most of us have similar feelings, because we are not used to having dogs as pets. I like pets, and I used to have at least one pet when I was a child. I had a cat, a turtle, love birds, fish, and sometimes a rabbit. But not a dog, it was considered as a disease causer, and its bite was harmful. Dogs are raised up as a guard or for hunt." My mom described.

"Showing your care for one's dog is kind of respect, as many people think. However, you don't have to get close to it or touch it, simply you can say that it's nice, but I prefer to stay away from dogs. People are going to understand and respect your choice." Noura's mom said.

Her answer spread peace for all of us. I really felt confused when a dog passed near me in the park, or when students at school talked about this subject.

Palmyra castle in the middle of Syrian

Nine

A GLIMPSE OF HOPE

The daily routine was getting easier to deal with. For us, as kids, the school was the biggest obstacle, maybe because we were faced by challenges away from our parents. Anyway, they weren't so far from us, because they always asked about each detail that happened with us at school to be sure that everything was going normal and fine.

Uncle Samir and his wife confirmed what we had heard about some students' violent behavior against each other. That was strange and unusual to happen at school by kids. My parents always reminded us to be polite by following all instructions, and to stay away from smoking, drugs, wrong relationships, and any other problems. I still couldn't exactly understand what they meant by those points! I knew that smoking and drugs were dangerous, but how could that happen in a school and how can a student pay for such things?

If we realized something was going wrong from our point

of view, my parents told us to mind our own business and not to interfere. Honestly, intervening in other people's privacy is wrong and unacceptable. Uncle Samir knows that it was a bad habit that was widespread in our country.

We did our best to make everything pass peacefully and to choose our words carefully, but sometimes things got hard to manage. At Majd's college during a writing class, he had to write an essay about one of his hobbies. He wrote a beautiful one about visiting new countries to explore and get to know new cultures. So, he ended his essay by saying that being a tourist guide was his hobby. When he read his subject in front of the teacher and the whole class, he made a spelling mistake by saying "terrorist" instead of a tourist. It was a dangerous mistake. Everybody understood what he wanted to say, but they couldn't hide their laughter. However, the teacher and the principal met with Majd and my parents. They wanted to know what he knew about this word, and its impact on him, and other related details. It took some time to clear up that this word was frequently repeated on TV, and it was just a pronunciation mistake. After that, Majd stayed for weeks mostly silent and lonely outside the home as much as he could to avoid similar situations.

A few days later, during a basket ball game, while I was playing with my class team, I slipped and hurt my leg! Directly, the coach called the nurse for help. She examined me and said that I needed to do an x-ray because my leg might be broken.

That was the last thing I expected. We had, at this period, many things to take care of. I felt worried about my dad since he held a huge responsibility. He worked overtime to meet our needs, and to cover the car payment he has bought after he obtained the driver's license. The car was an important thing that he needed. My dad is an ambitious person; he planned to work for his license diploma to improve our living status. I love him a lot. All of us respected and appreciated his efforts to give us a better life. I did not want to increase his suffering, but things sometimes happen.

The hospital exam result proved the nurse's expectation and showed that my leg was broken. My case required a small surgery, so I had to stay in the hospital for a few days. I was in a bad mood because the fear of surgery added another difficulty to the family. Besides all that, my leg hurt me. Doctors came in to check, they introduced their names and specialties. They told us their opinion about my case. Medical words were new to me, so I couldn't understand what they said. "being a refugee is ugly, I hate myself. Always there is suffering, and difficulties." I thought.

While I was thinking this way, a doctor was talking to my father and realized that I was upset. She dragged a chair towards me, sat down, looked at me with a big nice smile, and asked me:

"How do you feel now, sweetie?"

"Not bad!" I replied.

She kindly explained my case, and the procedures they were going to do to treat my leg. She said that it was easy and everything will be okay. I said nothing.

"So, are you happy to be in the US?" She asked. I nodded.

"You know, I came with my family to the US a long time ago from China as a refugee." She stated.

She had a non-American figure. I don't like to tell someone that I am a refugee, I don't like this word. She was a nice and beautiful doctor, how could she say that about herself?

"My family had to go abroad looking for a better living condition. We had bad and hard times when we first came here. In the past, things were harder than now. There was no easy social communication with the rest of the family in our country, which was hard. Being a refugee is not shameful or bad. It is a period we were forced to live for some reason." She said, as she felt what I was thinking about.

"How could you bear all the problems and became a successful woman?" I interestingly asked.

"I didn't consider difficulties as problems. I count them as challenges and I have to be patient to win. And I set up my target to be a doctor then I did all my best."

She left, but her words helped me to recall my grandmother's words, Boukra-Ahla.

Jasmine flowers

Ten

KEEP GOING

Spring has started. I took the cast off my leg. Five weeks passed since I broke my leg, and I have totally recovered.

I felt happy and lucky for all the support I got from family, friends, and doctors. However, I was feeling that I had a "lump" deep in my heart. I wasn't sure about the reason; it felt like something was missing.

Until now, everything was going as usual. My dad was working hard for his license diploma, and he was still in the same job, but he was expecting to get a better one. Mom had learned many new things to manage with the American's life style as well as her English language has improved. She was still attending her ESL classes. She planned to get a job as a teacher assistant at a nursery. Majd, Amal, and I had almost got by with our school matters.

With the ending of the school term, and approaching the summer season, there was going to be a big meeting in the

Mosque after two weeks. All of us were glad to hear this news. We really needed it because we had a busy and stressful semester.

During the winter, we attended some meetings. Those were like discussion meetings about new comers' issues. This time, I felt it was going to be different. It will be like a festival or a celebration that was the expectation for the majority of kids.

It was about time! There were many people we already knew. I saw Aunt Samia. There were some new people with her, and they looked like new comers that she was helping. It has been a long time since I last saw her, though she kept in contact with my parents. The meeting organizers were talking and discussing some important subjects as usual. The kids stayed outside in the yard in groups; playing, walking, or talking.

This area in America is usually foggy on most days of the year. Today was sunny, that was what we needed and missed. The sun was the first thing I talked about with the group who chose to sit and talk while enjoying the sunshine.

"I have never thought I may miss the sun some day! Have you?" I said.

"Yes, I agree with you, Yasmine. I used to know that clouds are gathering in the sky just when it is going to rain, which happened in my country. And it rained only in the winter." Mariam replied.

I have met this girl here at the first meeting. Last time, she was shy and mostly stayed silent.

She continued: "The Middle Eastern countries are known as-"the sunshine countries"-, my city is almost located in a valley surrounded by mountains. I used to spend most of the time walking and climbing hills in the sunshine."

"Maloula is your country. It is near Damascus, the capital of

Syria, right?" I asked.

"Yes, It's a famous tourist place, it has an ancient Church. It is the only place in the world where people are still talking Aramaic language, it is Jesus' language."

I've been there once on a school trip when I was in the sixth grade. But I never been to Aleppo, Karim talked about it, and I saw a video on YouTube. The video described many beautiful roads and places. I would have liked to go there. Most of it has turned to ruins now.

Lunch time started. We enjoyed a delicious variety of meals from different countries. My mother called me to introduce me to a lady and her daughter, who sat next to her. They are from Yemen. I knew this country was far away from Syria, but I know that this country had a wonderful, special building style and very old history. It suffers from war and very bad living conditions.

Later, Mouna, the Yemeni girl and I joined the kids' group outside. I thought she was shy or didn't like to talk, but a few minutes later she looked more relaxed and started telling us her news. Her father had a bad backache and had to stay lying down most of the time. Her mother was taking care of him and ran after the family home needs. Mouna's older brother worked hard to cover financial commitments.

Mouna was older than me. She had to attend college, but she was waiting for her family condition to get better, because she was afraid to use the bus alone, and needed some help at the beginning.

Majd told her regarding his experience with college and offered his help by lending her his books to prepare herself for next semester. I was happy to see her smile.

We exchanged interesting things about the memories we had

from our countries and the experience we got here.

Old Church at Maloula city

Eleven

HOME COUNTRY AROMA

Late in the evening while we were having tea. We discussed today's meeting. The most interesting news my father told us was that uncle Samir is traveling to Syria this summer!

This news triggered our feelings of being homesick. There was a pause of silence before my father said as he was staring in our eyes: "I can understand what you are thinking about! I know your feelings, because I had the same feeling when he told me that."

Nobody said a word. He looked at us and told us that uncle Samir was going to visit his parents, who lived with his brother.

"When I warned him about the bad condition of the war, he told me that the place he is going to reach is considered a safe area. Besides, his father is sick, and it has been a long time since he last saw his parents." Dad said, and added his opinion: "keeping in touch via the internet is very helpful, but it is not the same as meeting face to face from time to time."

At this moment, I had mixed emotions. From one side; missing the past with all the good and bad memories I spent with people and places I love. On the other hand, I liked to have a better future in a safe country that had ample opportunities for us. Now, I've realized the reasons for the "lump" I had in my heart. They are the fogginess and confusion of my feelings.

"Confused and sad feelings that all immigrants have usually subsided after the first visit back to the home country." Dad said, and explained: "Mostly, when we leave our home country, we just focus on the good memories, and automatically avoid the bad ones. So, when we suffer from changing our habits, we miss good things we left behind."

Dad talked about uncle Samir's experience as he got from his talk this morning. Uncle Samir expected to find everything exactly the same when he left Syria the first time. When he got there, he found things were running as usual before he moved to America. Most people were busy or had something to do, but he felt that his place was different in some way. He had no routine work to do; as a job, or regular missions. He missed the place that he had started there in the new home country. He enjoyed his time just as a trip.

After his first trip, he came back full of energy and passion for continuing his job and normal life. Another good advantage he realized that the second arrival to the US was different than the first time. This was because he already got engaged with new things, and there was no need for help. Doing things by himself was not an obstacle anymore. Since that time, he decided to go there when it was possible to visit his family and country.

"We will go there to visit our family, spend some time and recharge our energy when it is possible, I promise." Dad said.

Later, at the end of this discussion, my Dad's parents joined us via Skype. Dad told them about uncle Samir trip and our comments. My grandfather agreed with Dad's analyses, and added that the individual has to make an intention to be blessed anywhere and anytime.

"A good person should think about Jesus' words as the holy Quran has mentioned: "He (God) has made me blessed wherever I am [7]." Grandfather said, and explained: "You should get knowledge and benefit others in one hand and work for support and help yourself and the community as needed on another hand, anywhere you are to be blessed."

That night when I went to sleep, I reflected on the conversation that I heard. I remembered my grandma's stories about hope. I have found that made sense and made things clearer to me. That gave me a good feeling and support that I needed. I had decided to send the diary that I wrote to my grandma with uncle Samir. I am going to make the final touch and give it a title: "Boukra Ahla".

The Great Mosque of Damascus (Omayad Mosque)

GLOSSARY

1. Teta: grandmother in Arabic informal language.
2. Yasmine: Jasmine in Arabic language. Arabic people like to name their children names that have meaning of flowers, beauty, strength, glory, etc...
3. Jiddo: grandfather in Arabic language.
4. Boukra Ahla: It is a famous Syrian expression that means: tomorrow will be more beautiful.
5. Fashkoula:(Arabic word) a person who does a stupid action.
6. Rose Damask: This is a famous Syrian flower, originating from Damascus. People extract oil from it for perfumes, make rose water, and use their edible petals for garnish or tea.
7. Holly Quran. Chapter 19 Surat Marie verses

About the Author

Hiba Koueifi was born to a Syrian father and a Lebanese mother, in Damascus, the Syrian capital where she spent the days of childhood and the beginnings of her youth happily and safely in a family that loves and supports education and work. In the 1980s, she got married and moved to reside in Beirut, the capital of Lebanon. She continued her education there, where she studied law and completed specialization in the fundamentals of Islamic jurisprudence, and she also taught Arabic from time to time. She has some unpublished writings. This was during the Lebanese Civil War. She lived through the meanings of the war, which was intensifying at times, so she sought refuge with her family in her first homeland, Syria. The war faded at times, and life returned as if nothing had happened.

The writer was among the few lucky Syrians who neither experienced the Syrian war nor asylum, but had previously experienced a similar experience in the Lebanese Civil War.

Although the Lebanese war ended in the 1990s, the

country continued to suffer from instability, so the family decided to move to America and live there, then to face the difficulties of living in foreign county with all challenges of different culture, traditions, and daily living requirements. This may have caused tension and confusion. In addition, the English language was another important challenge, which the writer did not master as the accent of the Pittsburgh area was not an easy thing. During the journey of adapting to the new situation, the writer received a lot of cooperation and positive understanding from the American citizens who she dealt with. Since then, she felt their love to accept and support others, while she understood the reasons for others' reluctance to do so.

As is the case for many people of the countries in which she grew up, the author loves optimism and likes to spread hope wherever and whatever the circumstances are. She hopes that she will be successful in her awaiting endeavors.

Made in the USA
Columbia, SC
08 August 2020